Gabe's Busy Day

By
Roger Priddy

Gabe, Teddy, and Wallace are best friends.

Gabe is five years old.
So is Teddy.

Wallace is a dog.
He is very friendly.

Gabe lives with his family in a big city.

Today Gabe is going to school for the first time.

He tried on all kinds of different clothes.

He was excited as he set off with his mom.

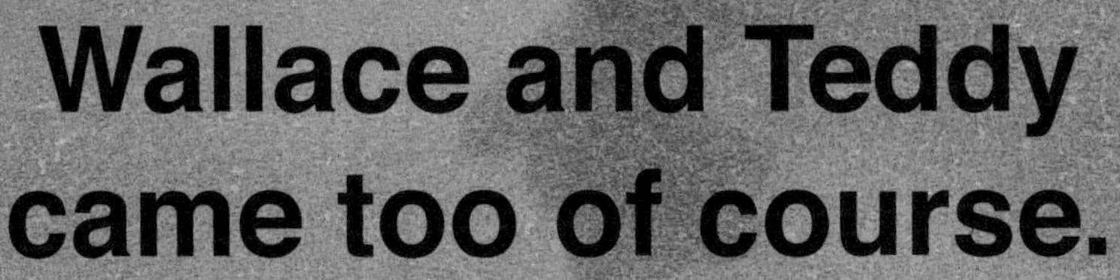

Wallace and Teddy
came too of course.

Gabe said hello to his new school principal.

When he waved goodbye,
Wallace howled!

Mom, Wallace, and Teddy went back home.

Wallace and Teddy were bored without their friend.

Meanwhile, at school
Gabe started playing.

This was fun. He started to make new friends.

Then Gabe painted
a picture.

And made a model.

He had lunch with
his new friends.

After lunch, his teacher read them a story.

Then they had
a little nap.

By the time school finished, Gabe didn't want to leave.

He was having so much fun.

Mom gave him Teddy.
He hugged him.

And Wallace too.
The three friends were
back together again.

After dinner, Gabe went to
the park with his dad.

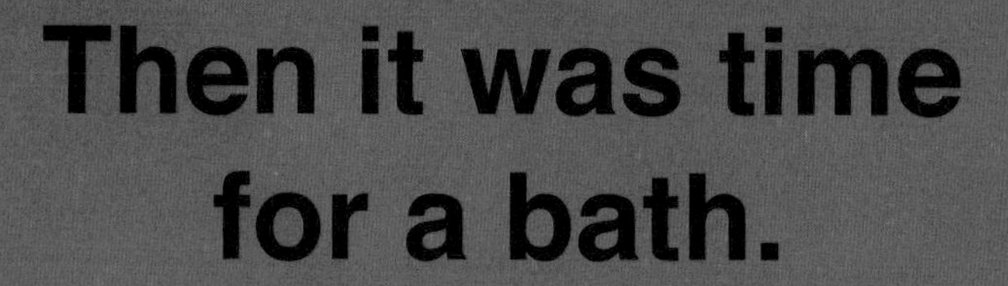

Then it was time
for a bath.

Oh no! Wallace got in too.
"Naughty dog!"

Wallace was very wet
when he got out.

He was sent outside
to dry off.

Gabe went to bed and dreamed of more adventures at school.

Where's Teddy?

By
Roger Priddy

Gabe, Wallace, and Teddy are best friends.

Teddy is a bit scruffy.

Wallace is always hungry.

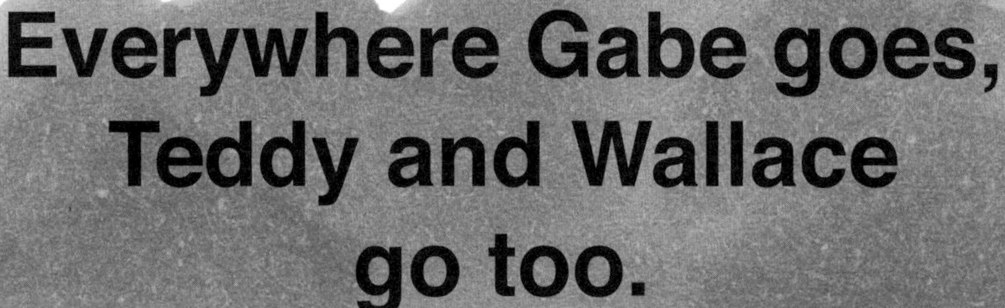

Everywhere Gabe goes,
Teddy and Wallace
go too.

They sit at the table.

They jump on the trampoline.

They ride in the car.

They even have a
bath together.

When Teddy isn't around, Gabe asks, "Where's Teddy?"

When Gabe
is tired,
"Where's
Teddy?"

When Gabe
falls over,
"Where's Teddy?"

Sometimes, Dad has
to fix Teddy.

If he smells bad, Dad puts him in the wash.

One day, Gabe goes to the park with Wallace.

They climbed trees and
played on the swings.

Gabe had an ice cream.

Wallace did too.

Then Gabe let out a yell,
"Where's Teddy?"

Mom, Dad, and Wallace looked at each other. Oh no! Teddy was lost!

Dad ran off with Wallace
to look for Teddy.

But they couldn't find him anywhere.

Mom searched
the house.

Wallace looked in his bed.

Mom gave Gabe his giraffe.

But all he could say was, "Where's Teddy?"

Suddenly, Wallace jumped up and down.

He knew where Teddy was.

Dad had left him in the dryer!

The three friends were back together.

And Gabe dreamed of another adventure.

Wallace the Hungry Dog

By
Roger Priddy

Gabe, Teddy, and Wallace
are best friends.

Wallace is a friendly dog.
He is always hungry.

Wherever Gabe is,
Wallace is always there.

If Gabe is in the bath,

Wallace gets in too!

Gabe and Wallace love the park.

Today they are playing on the swings...

...and splashing in the mud!

But all this exercise makes Wallace very hungry.

Wallace loves food more than anything else.

He looks for something to eat wherever he is.

He even chases after people if they have food!

"Naughty dog!"

He eats the fruit that Dad is growing.

"Wallace! No!"

And even the rotten apples that fall off the tree.

Then he has a
tummy ache...

...and is sick. This gets him into big trouble!

Gabe thinks that if Wallace is full then he won't eat bad things.

So he decides to feed him more dog food!

But Wallace just eats everything he is given.

And ends up very fat.

Now Wallace can't chase people in the park...

...or play fun games
with Gabe and Teddy.

Gabe is sad. He hadn't meant to make Wallace fat.

So he takes him to the vet, who says, “Less food and more exercise.”

Gabe sets about getting Wallace fit again.

They go for a run...

...a bicycle ride,

and a swim!

At last the three friends
are having fun again!

Wallace is a healthier dog ... but he still dreams about food!

Boys on Safari

By
Roger Priddy

Gabe, Wallace the dog, and Teddy are best friends.

Gabe's favorite book is about giraffes.

He wanted to go and find one in the park.

The three explorers packed for their journey.

They got to the park and began their search.

Wallace saw
a squirrel,
and
chased it.

“Naughty dog!”

Gabe climbed a tree to see if he could find a giraffe.

No giraffe, but he did find a bird on a nest.

And Wallace
found a
butterfly.

From the tree they could see a duck pond.

But where were the giraffes?

The three friends rowed across the pond.

A dragonfly flew past.

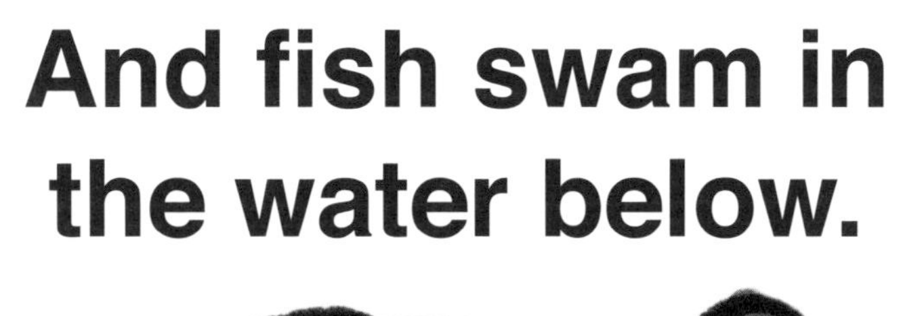

And fish swam in the water below.

They saw a duck looking for her ducklings.

Suddenly there was a big splash!

Wallace had seen a frog and jumped in. "Naughty dog!"

Wallace dried off and the friends had their picnic.

From the bushes they heard a noise:

"Quack, quack!"

They looked through the long grass.

Was it a giraffe?

No! They had found the lost ducklings.

Wallace carefully carried them back to the pond.

The ducklings were back with their mommy.

"Quack, quack!"

Gabe was sad not to find any giraffes, but happy to have returned the ducklings.

The three friends went home. It had been a long day.

They went to bed
and dreamed of more
adventures.

But he did make lots of friends.

And Dad said that was better than winning.

Sadly, Wallace was not one of them.

The judge picked the
three best dogs.
1st

And finally did something bad in the cup!

Everybody laughed.

Then he chewed one of the flowers.

And knocked over a vase of flowers and the cup.

He crashed into a table.

He jumped up and licked the judge.

But then Wallace started to howl!

Wallace was being very well behaved.

Gabe and Wallace lined up for the judge.

Gabe was excited.
Wallace was a bit nervous.

Finally it was time
for the show.

Wallace shook himself dry. Then Gabe brushed him.

On the day of the fair he gave Wallace a bath.

Gabe imagined Wallace winning the first prize.

He decided to enter Wallace.

Then one day, Gabe saw
a sign in the park.

And Wallace soon got the idea. The treats helped!

But they kept going.

But Wallace just wanted
to play and bark.

Mom sent them to dog
training school.

And doesn't come back when you call him!

Wallace runs away with the stick.

When Gabe throws sticks in the park,

He howls and howls.
It is very embarrassing.

Wallace hates being left alone.

Gabe, Teddy, and Wallace go everywhere together.

Wallace is a friendly dog.

Gabe, Teddy, and Wallace are best friends.

Wallace and the Dog Show

By
Roger Priddy